This book belongs to:

_____

_____

To Hana.
- P.A.

To my grandma PoPo, who taught my mom how to cook.
- O.C.

To Juan Agustin & Ian Mateo.
- J.C.

immedium
inspiring a world of imagination

Immedium, Inc.
P.O. Box 31846
San Francisco, CA 94131
www.immedium.com

www.liberumdonum.com

Text Copyright © 2017 Phil Amara & Oliver Chin
Illustrations Copyright © 2017 Juan Calle

First hardcover edition published 2017.

Edited by Eric Searleman
Book design by Joy Liu-Trujillo

Printed in Malaysia
10 9 8 7 6 5 4 3 2 1

Library of Congress Cataloging-in-Publication Data

Names: Amara, Philip, author. | Chin, Oliver Clyde, 1969- author. | Calle, Juan (Illustrator), illustrator.

Title: The discovery of ramen / by Phil Amara & Oliver Chin ; illustrated by Juan Calle.

Description: First hardcover edition. | San Francisco : Immedium, Inc., [2017]. | Series: Asian hall of fame

Summary: Dao, a red panda, guides Ethan and Emma, two school children, back into time
to discover how ramen was created in Japan and how the noodle soup became popular worldwide.

Identifiers: LCCN 2017022179 (print) | LCCN 2017012834 (ebook) | ISBN 9781597021395 (ebook) |
ISBN 1597021393 () | ISBN 9781597021340 (hardback) | ISBN 1597021342 (hardcover)

Subjects: | CYAC: Time travel--Fiction. | Ramen--Fiction. | Red panda--Fiction. | Pandas--Fiction. |
Japan--History--1868---Fiction. | BISAC: JUVENILE FICTION / People & Places / Asia.

Classification: LCC PZ7.A49153 (print) | LCC PZ7.A49153 Dis 2017 (ebook) |
DDC [E]--dc23 LC record available at https://lccn.loc.gov/2017022179

ISBN: 978-1-59702-134-0

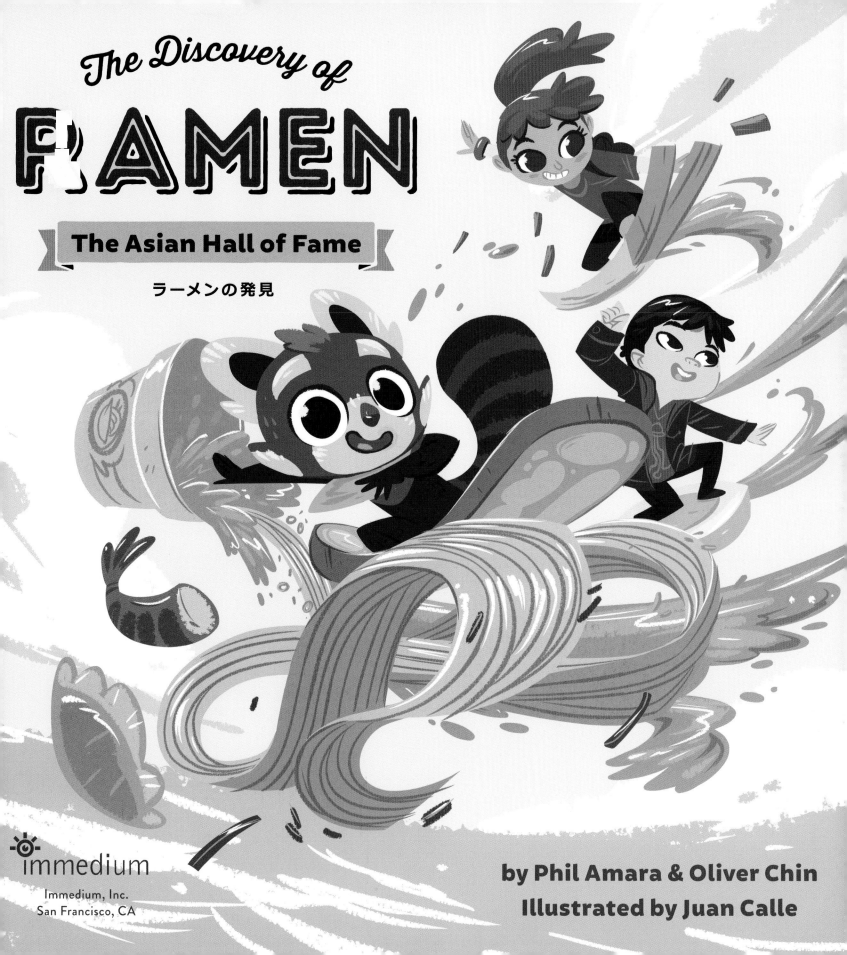

The Discovery of RAMEN

The Asian Hall of Fame

ラーメンの発見

immedium

Immedium, Inc.
San Francisco, CA

by Phil Amara & Oliver Chin

Illustrated by Juan Calle

A flavorful smell jolted Ethan and Emma.
The kids were exploring downtown
on a school field trip.

The savory scent tickled their noses and turned their heads.
As others shopped, the friends followed the aroma down the street.

They peeked inside a small restaurant.

People were busy eating hot noodle soup. Slurp!

Ethan's stomach grumbled. Emma's mouth watered.
Oh, they regretted bringing only peanut butter
and jelly sandwiches for lunch!

"What are they eating?"
wondered Emma.

"Whatever it is, I want some,"
sighed Ethan.

POOF!

"It's called *ramen*." Behind them stood a small red panda.
"My name is Dao You. But you can call me Dao."

"Who are you?" squealed Emma,
who loved cute critters.

Dao smiled. "I'm a guide to the
many fabulous creations from Asia -
inventions from food to fun!"

"Cool!" gushed Ethan,
who liked talking animals.

"Do you want to know how ramen came to be?" teased Dao.

Emma grabbed a notepad, and Ethan a fork. "Sure!" they replied.

Dao produced a small gong and mallet. "Gooone!"
Disappearing in a cloud of smoke, away they went!

The trio reappeared on a dusty path, lined with wooden buildings. Cars had vanished!

"Where are we?" asked Emma.

POOF!

"Where plus when!" answered Dao. "1880 in Yokohama, Japan!"

"Whoa!" muttered Ethan.

CHINA

JAPAN

PACIFIC OCEAN

"*Ramen* comes from the Chinese word *la mien*, which means pulled noodle," began Dao. "In northern China, noodles were made from wheat."

"So when Chinese came to Japan, they brought their food?" guessed Ethan.

"Yes! Street vendors sold noodle soup from pushcarts," stated Dao.

"The cook is attracting customers with a horn," noticed Emma.

"That's a *charumera*," Dao replied.
"Let's keep going." Zap!

They zipped ahead to Tokyo in 1910.
"Japan's capital city is bigger," proclaimed Dao.
"That means more businesses, more workers,
and more lunches to make."

"And more ingredients for ramen," drooled Ethan.

"This same year, Momofuku Ando was born in Taiwan," explained Dao. "Later he moved to Japan and became famous for popularizing 'instant' ramen."

CHINA

JAPAN

TAIWAN

"How'd that happen?" asked Ethan.

"I bet we'll find out," assured Emma.

Boom! Suddenly they were in 1945.
Tokyo looked gray and gloomy.
"World War II made life hard everywhere,"
whispered Dao.

"Like in other countries, Japan rationed food and restaurants closed."

"But after the war, the USA shipped tons of wheat to Asia.
Japan could bake more bread, like the West did.
But it also made ramen cheaper
to make and to buy."

"How is ramen made?"
asked Ethan.

"Good question!" responded Dao. "Let's see!"

Poof! They magically reappeared on an assembly line in a busy factory.
A mixer combined flour with salt, eggs, and water called *kansui*.

"Kansui is the special part," remarked Dao.
"It's like mineral water from a well."

"Does kansui make ramen springy?" asked Emma.

"Yellow, too?" added Ethan.

"You catch on quick!" smirked Dao.

The dough was kneaded, flattened, and stretched into a sheet
as thin as a dime! Next the sheet was cut into strands.
The noodles got their wavy shape so they wouldn't stick together.
Then they got a quick and hot steam bath.

SSHH!

"Ramen replaced *soba* ("buckwheat" in Japanese) as Japan's favorite noodle," Dao said.

"Remember Momofuku Ando? He became rich but had lost his fortune after the war.
Now could Ando become the king of ramen?"

"Ando seasoned the ramen so customers didn't have to," Dao said.
"Then he experimented frying the noodles in a flash."

"Hmm...dried noodles could last even longer than frozen ones!" predicted Emma.

SIZZLE!

Fast forward to 1958! "Ando sold his *chikin* ramen," announced Dao. "It became a hit and 30 years later his company promoted its birthday August 25th as Ramen Day."

Ethan licked his lips. "Chicken... Yum!"

Dao banged his gong again. "Gooone" to 1971!
"Now Ando put ramen in a cup," Dao explained.
"You didn't even need a pot, stove, or kitchen to eat it.
Cup O' Noodles contained dried vegetables and simple instructions."

Emma read:
1. Open lid

2. Add boiling water

3. Close lid for three minutes

4. Stir and eat

Dekiagari! A one-cup meal! "That was fast food before the microwave!" admired Ethan. "Can we learn more?"

Poof! Time-traveling to 1990, they visited ramen museums, which let them sample ramen from Japan's many regions. The toppings were many, too! "Roast pork, bamboo shoots, and scallions," observed Emma.

NARUTO

AJITAMA

UMEBOSHI

WHOOSH!

"Fish cake, soft-boiled egg, and salty pickled plum!" exclaimed Ethan, as he rubbed his belly. Meanwhile, Japan exported ramen around the globe, along with *sushi*, video games, and *anime*.

"Our next stop is out of this world!" declared Dao.

"We're in outer space!" gasped Emma.

"In 2005 a Japanese astronaut ate ramen
on the U.S. space shuttle Discovery," laughed Dao.

"Can anyone hear you slurp out here?" inquired Ethan.

"Look out for more factoids!" shouted Dao.

- 100 billion instant noodles are sold annually.

- That's like everyone having 13 servings of ramen a year!

- If those packages were stacked end to end, the line would stretch back and forth from the moon 13 times!

"I'll skip the bacon, pizza, or taco flavors," winced Ethan.

Zoom to today! The trio whisked across America. "Japan has 35,000 ramen shops. New ones pop up every day in other countries, too," yelled Dao. "Now it's like the beginning... more and more people like eating fresh ramen."

In New York the restaurant Momofuku named itself after Ando.
Other *ramen-ya* boast of handmade noodles, secret sauces,
and celebrity chefs trained in Japan. In every city,
diners debate which places serve the best dishes!

"The key is the broth. The delicious flavor is called *umami!*" explained Dao.
"Rich and savory, this is the fifth taste that people can sense."

"Aha, it's like the flavor from cheese, meat, mushrooms, or seaweed," inferred Emma.

Cooks put special seasonings called *tare* at the bottom of a bowl to give the broth different flavors. Common soups include:

SHIO
(SALT)

TONKOTSU
(PORK
BONE)

SHOYU
(SOY
SAUCE)

MISO
(SOY BEAN PASTE)

"Ooh, when can we try some?"
cried Ethan.

"Today anyone can share reviews, recipes, and photos of their favorite dishes," added Emma.

"That's oodles of noodles," slobbered Ethan.

"You don't have to be an expert to make ramen or wait in line to eat it," said Dao.

"Ramen can be a 25¢ dinner," commented Ethan.

SIZZLE!

"Or a slow cooked, comfort food," noted Emma.

"That reminds me of home... Oops it's time we go back!" yelped Dao.
The children had forgotten about their class field trip!

"Gooone!" They reappeared downtown.
"Wow, it's the same time as when we left!" exclaimed Ethan.

"I hope you enjoyed our trip!" grinned Dao. "Ramen's tale has as many twists as the noodles themselves. *Sayonara!*"

"Thanks! We'll see you again soon!"
gushed Emma. The bus was waiting,
but she couldn't leave just yet.
"Ethan, where are you?"

SOY SAUCE

Back in the restaurant, Ethan lifted his chopsticks to a big bowl of ramen. Slurp!

GLOSSARY

Ajitama — soft-boiled egg (Japanese)

Anime — animation (Japanese)

Charumera — horn used by 1880s noodle vendors to attract customers (Japanese)

Chashu — roast pork (Japanese), "Char siu" in Chinese

Chikin — chicken (Japanese)

Dao You — tour guide (Chinese)

Dekiagari — "Voila! Ready!" (Japanese)

Kansui — alkaline water that makes ramen noodles springy and yellow (Japanese)

La Mien — pulled noodle (Chinese)

Momofuku Ando — founder of Nissin, which makes instant ramen (his Chinese name is Bai-fu)

Miso — soybean paste flavored ramen (Japanese)

Naruto — fish cake (Japanese)

Ramen — Japanese noodle soup; noodles are made from wheat flour (Japanese)

Ramen Day — August 25th is when Nissin sold chikin ramen in 1958

Ramen-ya — ramen restaurant (Japanese)

Sayonara — "Goodbye" (Japanese)

Shio — salt flavored ramen (Japanese)

Shoyu — soy sauce flavored ramen (Japanese)

Soba — thin, gray colored noodles made from buckwheat flour (Japanese)

Sukari — scallions (Japanese)

Sushi — bite-sized pieces of vinegared rice with seafood and/or vegetables (Japanese)

Takenoko — bamboo shoots (Japanese)

Tare — seasoning base of broth for ramen soup (Japanese)

Tokyo — capital of Japan

Tonkotsu — pork bone flavored ramen (Japanese)

Umami — rich and savory flavor, the fifth taste after sweet, sour, salty, and bitter ("delicious taste" in Japanese)

Umeboshi — salty picked plum (Japanese)

Yokohama — city south of Tokyo, one of Japan's first ports opened to foreign trade in 1859

Fun Fact: Now China buys 8 times more instant ramen than Japan every year.